OUR FAMILY

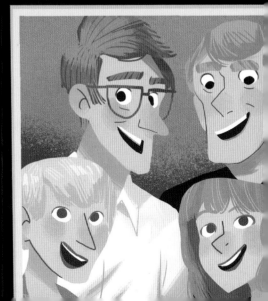

With happy memories of the many gatherings at the home of Bob and Donna Hicks,
where the welcome mat was always out. —L. A.

For my mom and dad, and Eric. —K. S.

STERLING CHILDREN'S BOOKS
New York

An Imprint of Sterling Publishing
1166 Avenue of the Americas
New York, NY 10036

STERLING CHILDREN'S BOOKS and the distinctive Sterling Children's Books logo are trademarks
of Sterling Publishing Co., Inc.

Text © 2015 by Linda Ashman
Illustrations © 2015 by Kim Smith
The artwork for this book was created digitally.
Designed by Andrea Miller

ISBN 978-1-4549-1024-4

Distributed in Canada by Sterling Publishing
c/o Canadian Manda Group, 664 Annette Street
Toronto, Ontario, Canada M6S 2C8
Distributed in the United Kingdom by GMC Distribution Services
Castle Place, 166 High Street, Lewes, East Sussex, England BN7 1XU
Distributed in Australia by Capricorn Link (Australia) Pty. Ltd.
P.O. Box 704, Windsor, NSW 2756, Australia

For information about custom editions, special sales, and premium and corporate purchases,
please contact Sterling Special Sales at 800-805-5489 or specialsales@sterlingpublishing.com.

Manufactured in China
Lot #:
2 4 6 8 10 9 7 5 3 1
7/15

www.sterlingpublishing.com/kids

Over the River & Through the Wood

A HOLIDAY ADVENTURE

by Linda Ashman • illustrated by Kim Smith

STERLING CHILDREN'S BOOKS
New York

Come to our house for the holidays - and bring your favorite pie!

Love,
Grandma & Grandpa

Pack up the pooches and load the van.
We need to leave by eight!
There's so much to bring.
Do we have everything?
Come on, we can't be late!

Into the tunnel, across the bridge,
Beyond the overpass.
Dad mumbles, "Uh, oh.
The fuel gauge is low.
Looks like we need some gas."

Mile after mile on two-lane roads,
No stations along the way.
No gas—not a drop.
We sputter, then stop.
We start to walk, then . . .

NEXT
SERVICE
STATION

20 MILES

Into the lobby and out the door.
The subway's down the street.
A crowded ride;
We're squished inside.
Hey—ouch!—you're on my feet!

Race through the station to catch the train.
Quick! It's leaving soon.
The gray city scene
Turns to white and green.
We should be there by noon.

Arrive at the depot; we scramble out.
We're almost there—hooray!
The house isn't far,
But there's no rental car.
We head down the road, then . . .

Off to the airport before the dawn.
It's park, then dash, then . . . wait.
We coil and wind
In a serpentine line.
At last—we're at the gate!

Over the mountains, above the plains,
The buildings disappear.
Then we circle around
And we're back on the ground.
We'll take the bus from here.

Beyond the village and past the farm,
The shuttle begins to sway.

A flat! Bad luck.
No spare. We're stuck.
Hey, what's that sound? A . . .

Around the harbor and up the coast,
Through the waves and the salty air.
We head for the dock.
Look out for that rock!
Whew! We're halfway there.

Climb in the basket, release the ropes,
And into the sky we rise.
We float with the breeze,
Above houses and trees.
Hey, wait—where are the pies?

Drifting past forests and toward the fields,
We land beside some hay.
It's not far to go;
We'll trudge through the snow.
But then . . .

      You guessed it . . .

Over the river and through the wood—
The horse is trotting fast.
The sleigh bells ring;
We laugh and sing.
To Grandma's house, at last!

Grandma is pacing and
Checking clocks.
"I hope they're all okay."
Says Grandpa, "They're fine—
Just a little behind."
And then they hear it . . .

Pull in the driveway and storm the porch.
The door swings open wide.
A whoop, a cheer,
And a "Look who's here!"
It sure smells good inside.

Haul in the duffles, unpack the pies,
And thaw our frosty feet.
We play and chat.
The dogs chase the cat.
Then Grandpa calls, "Let's eat!"

Elbow to elbow, we gather 'round,
With thanks for our happy day—
For family, for pie,
For homes, warm and dry,
For friends . . .

. . . and a horse-drawn sleigh.

Neighhhh!